DUE

I WAS SO SICK

BY GINA AND MERCER MAYER

Westport, Connecticut

Published by Reader's Digest Young Families, Inc. Printed in the U.S.A. LITTLE CRITTER® is a registered trademark of
Mercer Mayer. READER'S DIGEST KIDS & DESIGN is a registered trademark of The Reader's Digest Association, Inc.
ISBN: 0-89577-778-9

Last night I woke up with a tummy ache.
I called Mom. She said I had a fever.

She put a cool washcloth on my head and
rubbed my tummy. I was so sick.

Mom sat beside my bed
and held my hand all night.

In the morning I was still sick. I didn't have to go to school, but even that didn't make me happy. I'd rather go to school than be so sick.

Mom said, "We need to go to the doctor to get some medicine for your tummy."

I didn't want to go to the doctor, but I wanted to feel better. So I was brave.

There were lots of toys at the doctor's office,
but I was so sick I didn't play with any of them.

A pretty nurse took us to a room. I sat on a bed covered with paper.

Then the doctor came in.
He had big ears.
But he had a nice smile.

He asked the nurse to
take my temperature.
I only had a little fever.

He put a stick in my mouth,
and told me to say, "Aahh."
I thought that was weird.

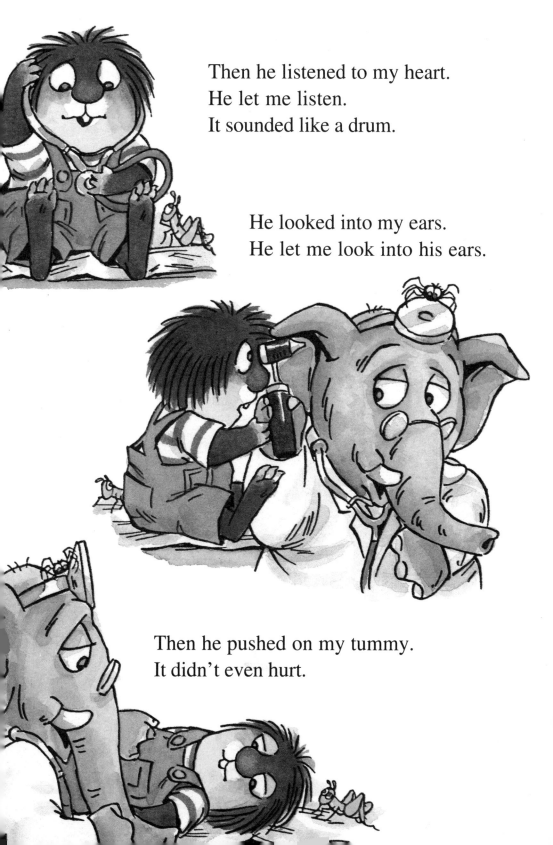

Then he listened to my heart.
He let me listen.
It sounded like a drum.

He looked into my ears.
He let me look into his ears.

Then he pushed on my tummy.
It didn't even hurt.

The doctor gave my mom a prescription for some medicine. He said it would make my tummy as good as new.

He shook my hand. "You were a very good patient," he said. I got a big red balloon.

We went to the drugstore to get my medicine.
I was so sick, I forgot to ask for a new toy.

When we got home, Mom made me
take my medicine. "Yuck!"

Then I lay down on the couch to watch cartoons.
I went to sleep by accident.

When I woke up, I started to cry
because I had missed my cartoons.

But my tummy felt better.
That doctor was so smart!

When Dad came home, I told him all about the
doctor and the pretty nurse. "You're such a brave
critter," he said.

Then he read me a story and put me to bed.

Dad says I'll probably be all better tomorrow.
Boy, I sure hope so.